THE
Bread
GET

...ough Story

ILLUSTRATED BY
Nelleke Verhoeff

It seemed like I'd been waiting forever for my uncle to visit again.

"Mum! Mama!" I shouted. "Look!"

They waved to JB's rusty camper as it stopped. I ran to greet him.

"Hey, Butterbean," he said. "Thought I'd stop in on my way out west. Could you look after something for me while I'm gone?"

"Of course!" I said. "You know I love your goldfish."

"Not just Poquito," he replied.

"Cora, meet my Bread Pet," said JB. "It's sourdough, with bacteria and fungi growing inside it."

"GROSS!" I backed away.

"Gross and awesome!" exclaimed JB. "Bacteria and fungi are alive. They eat the dough and change it. The fungi make it rise up light and fluffy. The bacteria give it a nice sour taste."

I took a closer look at the goo. "So it's really alive?"

JB showed me how to stir water and flour into the Bread Pet to feed it.

FLOUR

"It's called starter because you can use it to start a new loaf of sourdough bread," he explained. "Until you're ready to bake, keep feeding it. It gets hungry twice a day."

JB gave me a note with instructions, then frowned. "I feel like there's something I'm forgetting to tell you," he said.

I shrugged. "Seems pretty easy!"

Feeding the Bread Pet turned out to be a lot of work.
I had to measure the sticky Bread Pet and the flour
and the water, making sure I had the amounts
right and trying not to make a mess.

FEED
BREAD PET
HALF ITS WEIGHT
IN WATER
+ HALF IN
FLOUR
—J.B.

FLOUR

C

The first day, I tried to give the job to someone else.
Mum said, "No way." Mama just laughed. None of
us knew how soon things would get out of control.

It only took a couple of days for the Bread Pet to outgrow the biggest mixing bowl in the house. Mum suggested we move it to a bucket. Mama split it into two containers, and then four, and then eight. We had flour in our hair and Bread Pets oozing all over the kitchen.

How did the Bread Pet grow so quickly?
If one bowl turns into two bowls, then...

I started drawing.

I couldn't even write the next line without running off the page. I tried to imagine what the kitchen was going to look like in a few days. I gulped.

"Why does JB even keep this stupid Bread Pet!?" I grumbled to myself.

Mum stuck her head in the doorway. "He keeps it so he can bake bread, silly. Didn't you see the recipe on the back?" She waved JB's crumpled note at me.

"Do you think JB would mind if we baked some?" I asked.

"No," Mum said, laughing. "I think he'd like that."

So that's what we did. The first loaf was a little flat, but Mum said we'd get better at it with time.

Baking some of the Bread Pet didn't solve our problem. It was growing faster than we could bake.

"I am sick of all this mess," said Mama after a few days.

"I am sick of all this bread," I replied.

"You know," said Mum, "we might be sick of this bread, but there are a lot of people who would be thankful to have something like this to eat."

That gave me an idea.

I asked Mum if she'd help me bake one more loaf to share. It turned out perfectly — golden and puffy, with a heavenly smell. We sliced it carefully and wrapped it up before we walked together to the community hall. The smell followed us up the road.

Our community hall was a busy swirl of people and sounds and food. The director, Toya, thanked us for our donation, and I watched my bread move through the room. It was passed around the tables of people, and just like that, it was *gone*.

"Are you okay, sweetie?" Toya asked.

I poked around in my brain for the right words.
"I just ... didn't think it would be gone so fast."

6

When we got home,
I went straight into the kitchen.
There were even more bowls
of oozy goo than I remembered.

"Argh, Poquito! I'm only one person.
I can't bake all this bread myself!"

Poquito opened and closed his little circle
mouth, and the Bread Pet just bubbled.
All of the Bread Pets just bubbled.

That gave me another idea.

"I thought of something else we can try," I said.

It took Mama, Mum and me all working together to load my wagon up with our gooey jars and containers. They rattled all the way to the community hall.

Toya looked a little surprised
to see us. "Cora!" she said.
"You're back!"

The next day, the cafeteria at the community hall was full.

Toya and I taught everyone about Bread Pets and how to care for them — and of course, how to bake the bread. Toya even knew some things I didn't, like that Bread Pets grow much more slowly if you keep them in the fridge. (I wish we'd known *that* sooner!)

Toya asked if anyone had a question for us. At the back of the class, someone raised their hand.

"Hey, Butterbean!" said a familiar voice.

"Did I forget to tell you to put it in the fridge?"

Make Your Own Bread Pet

Day 1: Mix

1. Place an empty jar on a kitchen scale and set the scale to zero.
2. Add 100 g (⅚ cup, or ½ + ⅓ cup) of flour and 100 g (about ⅖ cup or 6 ½ tbsp) of water to the jar.
3. Stir until all dry parts are mixed in.
4. Keep this mixture somewhere warm, between 70°F to 75°F (21°C to 24°C), but out of direct sunlight.

Day 2: Feed

1. Place another empty jar on the kitchen scale and set the scale to zero.
2. Scoop in 200 g (about 1 cup) of the mixture you made on Day 1. Compost or throw away the rest (this will make sure your Bread Pet stays a manageable size).
3. Add 100 g (⅚ cup, or ½ + ⅓ cup) of flour and 100 g (about ⅖ cup or 6 ½ tbsp) of water.
4. Mix well until all dry parts are mixed in.
5. Cover and place in the same warm spot as Day 1.
6. Repeat steps 1–5 daily for at least 5 days.

Congratulations, you've just created your own Bread Pet. Now you're ready to bake some bread!

You'll Need

- adult helper
- water (tap left out overnight or distilled works best)
- 700 g (about 6 cups) flour (rye or whole wheat works best)
- 2 clean glass jars
- kitchen scale (optional, but recommended for best results) or measuring cup

Note

Sourdough starters need a few days to ferment, or for the fungi and bacteria to produce the gases and acids that make the bread rise and give it its sour taste. They ferment faster in warm places and more slowly in cold ones.

Bread Pet Tips

- Keep your Bread Pet in a container with a loose-fitting lid so that it gets some air but doesn't completely dry out.
- Feed your Bread Pet daily or keep it in the fridge if you want to feed it weekly instead. You can tell that your starter needs food when it is bubbling, at least twice its original size, and starting to collapse.
- If you don't want to throw away the extra when you feed your Bread Pet, you can add it to dough for pancakes, waffles or crackers to make them extra tangy.

Bake Bread!

Mix

1. Whisk the Bread Pet, water and olive oil in a large bowl. Add the flour and salt.
2. Squish everything together with your hands until all the flour is absorbed.
3. Let it rest for 30 minutes.
4. Collect the dough into a rough ball.

First Rise

1. Cover the bowl with a kitchen towel. Leave it in a warm, sunny spot to rise.
2. Wait for your dough to double in size (3–12 hours, depending on temperature).

Stretch and Fold

1. Place the dough on a clean, floured surface. Coat your hands with flour.
2. Grab the far end of the dough and pull it up, stretching it without breaking it. Fold it back on itself.
3. Repeat step 2, stretching from the left, right and near ends of the dough.
4. Flip the dough over.
5. Repeat steps 2–4 a few times.

Second Rise

1. Cover the bottom of your Dutch oven with parchment paper or coat it with cornmeal to prevent sticking.
2. Place the dough inside for a second shorter rise, about 1–2 hours. It is ready when the dough is slightly puffy.

Bake

1. Preheat the oven to 450°F/235°C.
2. With the serrated knife, make a shallow slash about 2 in (5 cm) long in the middle of the loaf. You can make a few slashes if you want.
3. Place your Dutch oven, with dough inside and lid on, into your preheated oven. Reduce the oven temperature to 400°F/205°C.
4. Bake for 20 minutes.
5. Remove the lid and continue to bake, uncovered, for an additional 40 minutes or until bread is a deep golden brown.
6. Remove the bread from the oven and let it cool for at least 1 hour before slicing. Don't cut too soon or else the inside will have a gooey texture!

You'll Need

- adult helper
- 150 g (1 cup) hungry Bread Pet
- 1 cup warm water (about 105°F/40.5°C)
- 2 tbsp olive oil
- 420 g (3 ½ cups) flour (bread flour works best)
- 1 tbsp salt
- parchment or greaseproof paper
- Dutch oven, casserole dish or heavy baking pot with lid
- kitchen towel
- serrated knife
- thermometer (optional)
- cornmeal (optional)

Baking Tips

- All ovens are a little different. You might have to make small adjustments to these times or temperatures.
- When the bread is done, its internal temperature should be at least 205°F/95°C.

Your Growing Bread Pet

Just like the Bread Pet in this book, your Bread Pet is alive. It is full of very small living things called microbes, which can be bacteria or fungi. When each microbe gets enough food, it doubles into two microbes. Each of those two doubles again, so then there are four microbes. Each of those four doubles, to make eight microbes. Eight microbes become 16. 16 become 32. The more microbes there are, the faster your Bread Pet grows!

More About Sourdough

Sourdough is well-known among bakers for being one of the most difficult types of bread to bake from scratch. If your first, second or even sixth batch of sourdough doesn't turn out the way you want, don't worry! You still learned something new every time you tried and bread can taste good even if it's not perfect.

You can learn a lot more about sourdough if you want to explore beyond this book. Here are some suggestions of books and websites to look for at your local library and on the internet:

- Forkish, Ken. *Flour Water Salt Yeast: The Fundamentals of Artisan Bread and Pizza.* Ten Speed Press, Berkeley, CA (2012).
- Hadjiandreou, Emmanuel. *Making Bread Together: Step-by-Step Recipes for Fun and Simple Breads to Make with Children.* Ryland Peters & Small, London (2014).
- *Sourdough Baking: The Complete Guide.* King Arthur Flour, Norwich, VT (2020). www.kingarthurflour.com

For Jeremy Barrett, the real JB. Forever my brother and my FFB — Kate
For Herman, my personal bread and pizza baker — Nelleke

The author would like to thank Michelle L. Trott for helping to ensure the accuracy of this book.

Barefoot Books
2067 Massachusetts Ave
Cambridge, MA 02140

Barefoot Books
29/30 Fitzroy Square
London, W1T 6LQ

This book was typeset in CamplandLetters, Cleanhouse and Tisa Mobi Pro
The illustrations were prepared digitally with handmade textures

Text copyright © 2020 Kate DePalma
Illustrations copyright © 2020 Nelleke Verhoeff
The moral rights of Kate DePalma and Nelleke Verhoeff have been asserted

Hardback ISBN 978-1-64686-064-7
Paperback ISBN 978-1-64686-065-4
E-book ISBN 978-1-64686-082-1

First published in the United States of America by Barefoot Books, Inc and in Great Britain by Barefoot Books, Ltd in 2020
All rights reserved

British Cataloguing-in-Publication Data:
a catalogue record for this book is available from the British Library

Graphic design by Sarah Soldano, Barefoot Books
Edited and art directed by Nivair H. Gabriel, Barefoot Books
Reproduction by Bright Arts, Hong Kong
Printed in China on 100% acid-free paper

Library of Congress Cataloging-in-Publication Data is available under LCCN 2020003036

1 3 5 7 9 8 6 4 2